CW00944941

This book belongs to

....

First published in 2014 by Miles Kelly Publishing Ltd
Harding's Barn, Bardfield End Green, Thaxted, Essex, CM6 3PX, UK

2 4 6 8 10 9 7 5 3 1

Publishing Director Belinda Gallagher
Creative Director Jo Cowan
Editor Fran Bromage
Senior Designer Joe Jones
Production Manager Elizabeth Collins
Reprographics Stephan Davis, Jennifer Hunt, Thom Allaway

ISBN 978-1-78209-488-3

Printed in China

British Library Cataloguing-in-Publication Data
A catalogue record for this book is available from the British Library

ACKNOWLEDGEMENTS
The publishers would like to thank the following artists
who have contributed to this book:
Cover (main): Jenny Arthur at The Bright Agency
Insides: Debbie Meekcoms

Made with paper from a sustainable forest

www.mileskelly.net   info@mileskelly.net

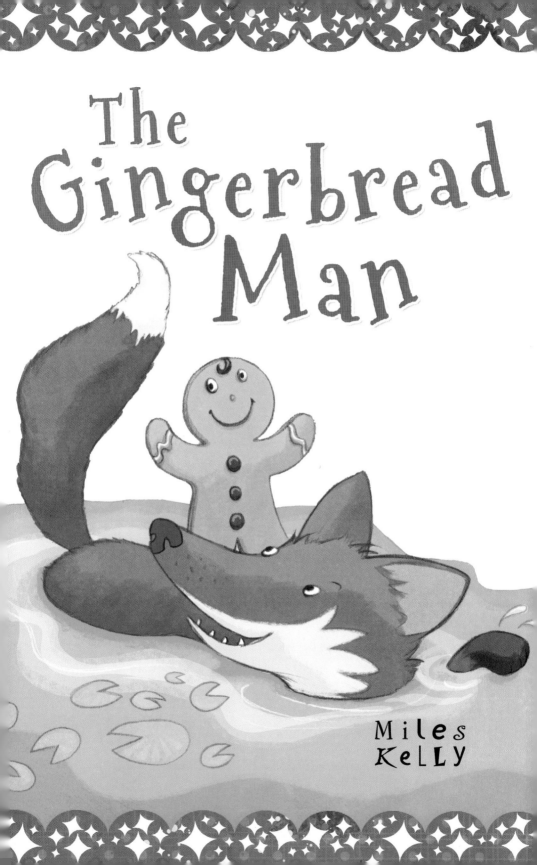

The Gingerbread Man

Miles Kelly

One fine sunny day, an old woman was baking in her kitchen. She was making ginger biscuits. As she had a bit of dough left over she

The Gingerbread Man

decided to make a little gingerbread man to give to her husband.

She gave the gingerbread man raisins for eyes, cherries for buttons and she put a smile on his little face with a piece of orange peel. Then

she popped the biscuits and gingerbread man in the oven.

A little while later, the old woman carefully lifted the tray out of the oven to check if the biscuits were cooked. Suddenly, the gingerbread man hopped off the tray and

The Gingerbread Man

Story time

The Gingerbread Man

ran straight out of the door!

The old woman ran after the gingerbread man, and hearing her shouts, the old woman's husband ran after her. But they couldn't catch the gingerbread man, who called out, "Run, run, as fast

as you can! You can't catch me, I'm the gingerbread man!"

Hearing the shouting, the old dog left his kennel and ran yapping after the old man and the old woman. But the dog couldn't catch the gingerbread man, who called

out, "Run, run, as fast as you can! You can't catch me, I'm the gingerbread man!"

The ginger cat, who had been asleep in the sun, ran yowling after the dog. But the cat couldn't catch the gingerbread man, who called

Story time

out, "Run, run, as fast as you can! You can't catch me, I'm the gingerbread man!"

The brown cow in the meadow ran after the cat. But the cow couldn't catch the gingerbread man, who called out, "Run, run, as fast

The Gingerbread Man

as you can! You can't catch me, I'm the gingerbread man!"

The black horse in the stable galloped after the cow. But the horse couldn't catch the gingerbread man, who called out, "Run, run, as fast as you can! You can't catch me, I'm the gingerbread man!" The fat pink pig in the sty trotted after the horse. But the pig couldn't catch the

The Gingerbread Man

gingerbread man, who called
out, "Run, run, as fast as you
can! You can't catch me,
I'm the gingerbread man!"
The cockerel flapped
and squawked after the pig.
But the cockerel couldn't
catch the gingerbread man,

Story time

who called out,
"Run, run, as fast
as you can! You can't catch
me, I'm the gingerbread man!"
The gingerbread man ran
and ran, and so the old
woman and the old man, the
dog and the cat, the cow and

16

The Gingerbread Man

the horse, the pig and the
cockerel all ran after him.
And he kept running until
he came to the river.

For the first time since he
had hopped out of the oven,
the gingerbread man
had to stop running.

"Help, help! How can I cross the river?" he cried. At that moment, a sly fox appeared by his side.

"I could carry you across," said the fox.

So, the gingerbread man jumped onto the fox's back

The Gingerbread Man

and the fox slid into the water. But after a short while, the gingerbread man said, "My feet are getting wet."

The fox just smiled, showing lots of very sharp teeth. "Well, jump onto my head," he said and kept swimming.

"My feet are still getting wet," said the gingerbread man again.

"Well, jump onto my nose,"

smiled the fox, showing even more teeth. So, the gingerbread man jumped onto the fox's nose, and SNAP! the fox gobbled him up.

When the fox climbed out onto the riverbank, all that was left of that naughty

gingerbread man was a few
crumbs. So, the old woman
and the old

man, the dog and the cat, the cow and the horse, the pig and the cockerel all went back home. And the old woman shared out the other ginger biscuits. They were delicious!

The End